MARION COUNTY PUBLIC L
321 MONROE STRE
FAIRMONT, WV 26554
P9-CLE-976

image comics presents

JUL 3 1 2013

ROBERT KIRKMAN
CREATOR, WRITER

CHARLIE ADLARD
PENCILER, INKER

CLIFF RATHBURN
GRAY TONES

RUS WOOTON
LETTERER

CHARLIE ADLARD
&
CLIFF RATHBURN
COVER

SEAN MACKIEWICZ
EDITOR

For SKYBOUND ENTERTAINMENT

Robert Kirkman - CEO
J.J. Didde - President
Sean Mackiewicz - Editorial Director
Shawn Kirkham - Director of Business Development
Brian Huntington - Online Editorial Director
Helen Leigh - Office Manager
Feldman Public Relations LA - Public Relations

For international rights inquiries,
please contact: foreign@skybound.com

WWW.SKYBOUND.COM

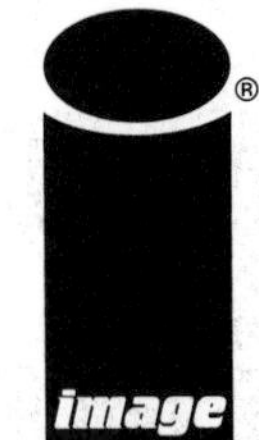

IMAGE COMICS, INC.
Robert Kirkman - chief operating officer
Erik Larsen - chief financial officer
Todd McFarlane - president
Marc Silvestri - chief executive officer
Jim Valentino - vice-president

Eric Stephenson - publisher
Ron Richards - director of business development
Jennifer de Guzman - pr & marketing director
Branwyn Bigglestone - accounts manager
Emily Miller - accounting assistant
Jamie Parreno - marketing assistant
Jenna Savage - administrative assistant
Kevin Yuen - digital rights coordinator
Jonathan Chan - production manager
Drew Gill - art director
Tyler Shainline - print manager
Monica Garcia - production artist
Vincent Kukua - production artist
Jana Cook - production artist
www.imagecomics.com

THE WALKING DEAD, VOL. 18: WHAT COMES AFTER. First Printing. Published by Image Comics, Inc. Office of publication: 2001 Center Street, 6th Floor, Berkeley, California 94704. Copyright © 2013 Robert Kirkman, LLC. All rights reserved. Originally published in single magazine format as THE WALKING DEAD #103-108. THE WALKING DEAD™ (including all prominent characters featured in this issue), its logo and all character likenesses are trademarks of Robert Kirkman, LLC, unless otherwise noted. Image Comics® and its logos are registered trademarks and copyrights of Image Comics, Inc. All rights reserved. No part of this publication may be reproduced or transmitted, in any form or by any means (except for short excerpts for review purposes) without the express written permission of Image Comics, Inc. All names, characters, events and locales in this publication are entirely fictional. Any resemblance to actual persons (living and/or dead), events or places, without satiric intent, is coincidental. For information regarding the CPSIA on this printed material call: 203-595-3636 and provide reference # RICH – 485676.

PRINTED IN THE USA

ISBN: 978-1-60706-687-3

WRAKK!

WHUDD!

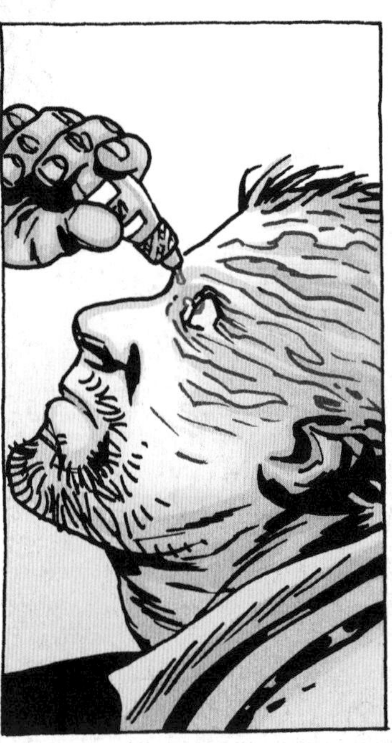

WRAKK!

WHAT IS THIS?

WHAT DOES IT LOOK LIKE? I'M MOVING OUT.
WHY?

DON'T ACT SURPRISED. WHAT DID YOU THINK WOULD HAPPEN? YOU'VE ABANDONED US AND THROWN US TO THE WOLVES!
I THOUGHT WE HAD AN OBLIGATION TO PROTECT THESE PEOPLE. YOU AND ME-- THE STRONG ONES... WE OWE IT TO THE OTHERS.
THERE ARE CHILDREN HERE... AND WE'RE JUST GOING TO... I CAN'T EVEN LOOK AT YOU...

...LET ALONE SLEEP NEXT TO YOU.

STOP.

I DON'T HAVE ANYTHING MORE TO SAY TO YOU.

I HAVE A PLAN.

WHAT? SURRENDER, LET THE BAD GUYS COME IN HERE AND TAKE WHATEVER THEY WANT?

THAT'S PART OF IT, YES.
BUT ONLY PART.

WHY WOULD YOU KEEP ME IN THE DARK?

FOR YOUR SAFETY. EVERYONE'S SAFETY.

I DON'T FOLLOW.

NEGAN AND HIS PEOPLE ARE GOING TO COME HERE. THEY'RE GOING TO PICK UP SUPPLIES AND THEY'RE GOING TO INTERACT WITH OUR PEOPLE.
YOU, CARL, HEATH, NICHOLAS, HOLLY, DENISE... EVERYONE.
THEY NEED TO BELIEVE THAT WE'RE SCARED, THAT WE'RE SUBMITTING, THAT WE HAVE NO PLANS TO RETALIATE IN ANY WAY. THEY NEED TO KNOW THEY HAVE US--AND THAT WE'RE GIVING UP.

BUT WE'RE NOT?

NO.
WE'RE NOT.

STAYING NOW?
YEAH.

I'M MAKING LUNCH.
YOU WANT A SANDWICH?

CARL?

DAMN IT, CARL.
LOOK AT ME.

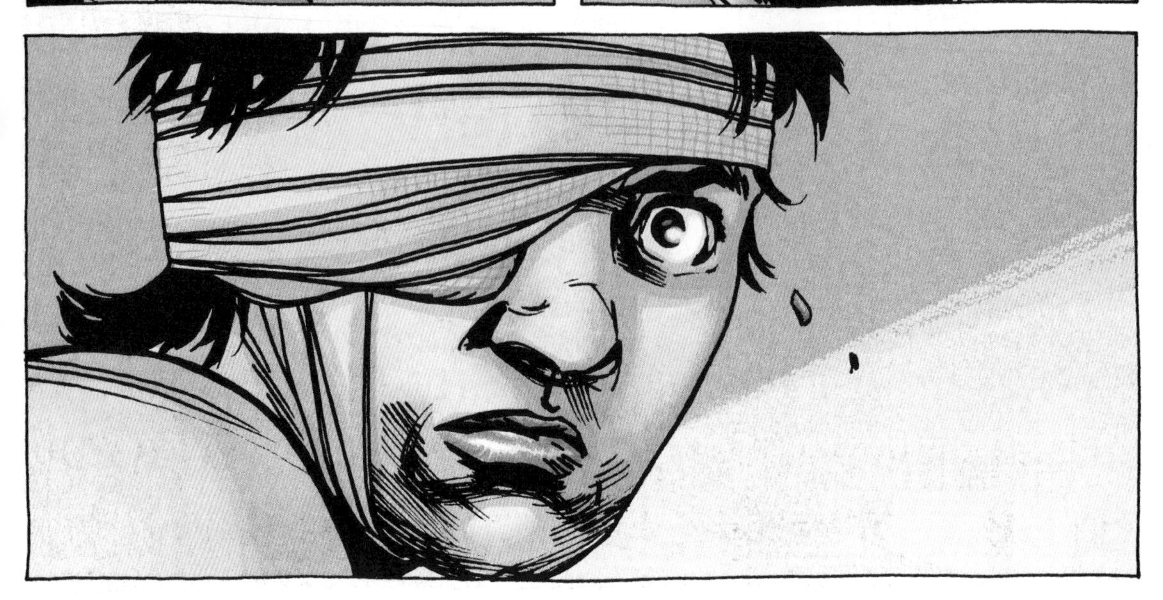

I UNDERSTAND WHY YOU'RE MAD. I DO.
I NEED YOU TO CUT ME SOME SLACK.

YOU'RE JUST A KID. I KNOW YOU HATE TO HEAR THAT, BUT IT'S TRUE. YOU NEED TO TRUST ME. I KNOW WHAT I'M DOING HERE.
THIS IS GOING TO WORK OUT. I KNOW IT DOESN'T SEEM LIKE IT, BUT EVERYTHING IS GOING TO BE FINE.

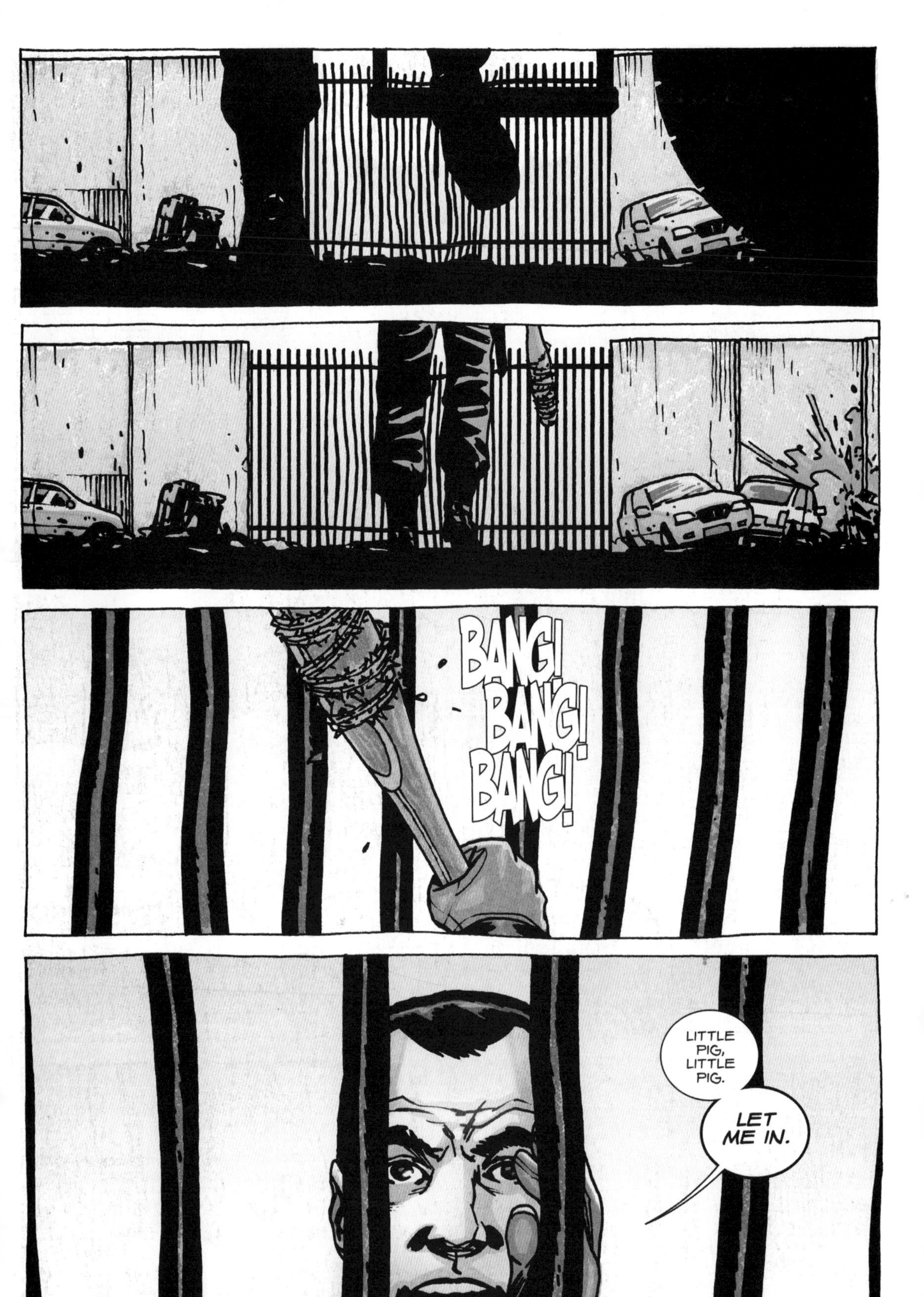
BANG!
BANG!
BANG!
LITTLE PIG, LITTLE PIG.
LET ME IN.

UM...
...WHO ARE YOU?

YOU BETTER BE FUCKING JOKING.
NEGAN?
LUCILLE?
I KNOW I HAD TO MAKE A PRETTY FUCKING STRONG FIRST IMPRESSION.
BUST A MOVE

TELL YOU WHAT. YOU GO FIND THAT GUY RICK AND TELL HIM NEGAN'S HERE. HE'LL KNOW WHAT TO DO.
IN THE MEANTIME, WE'LL TIDY UP OUT HERE A BIT. RUN ALONG, NOW.

SHUKK!

WRAMM!
FUCK.

WRAKK!

KRAKK!

HUFF!
HUFF!
OH.

HELLO THERE.
DON'T YOU MAKE ME HAVE TO FUCKING *ASK*.
OPEN IT UP.

YOU SEE THAT? NOW THAT IS SOME FUCKING SERVICE, AM I RIGHT? WE'RE ALMOST TURNED AWAY AT YOUR GATE--I MEAN, WHO IS THAT ASSHOLE, ANYWAY? DO I GET MAD? DO I THROW A FIT?
DO I BASH SOME POOR ASIAN KID'S FUCKING DOME IN?
NO. ME AND MY GUYS WAIT, BUT WHILE WE'RE DOING THAT... WE TAKE OUT A FEW OF THESE FUCKS, THESE DEAD FUCKS WHO COULD HAVE POSSIBLY KILLED ONE OF YOU.

MOTHER-FUCKING SERVICE.
HOLD THIS.

JUST LOOK AT THIS PLACE, IT'S MOTHERFUCKING COCKSUCKING MAGNIFICENT!
WOW!

YOU LIVE IN FUCKING HOUSES?! HOT DAMN, MAN. YOU'RE LIVING LIKE KINGS. HOW MANY YOU GOT HERE?
FORTY-NINE--FORTY-EIGHT.
NO SHIT? AND YOU GOTTA HAVE LIKE TWENTY HOUSES HERE. I BET YOU'VE EVEN GOT A FEW OF THESE FUCKERS EMPTY, DON'T YOU?
OF COURSE YOU DO. IT'S AN EMBARRASSMENT OF RICHES, AS THEY SAY.

YES, SIR. I DO BELIEVE YOU'LL HAVE PLENTY TO OFFER UP.

WELL, YOU GOING TO SHOW US AROUND OR NOT?

WELL?

WHAT WOULD YOU LIKE TO SEE FIRST?

MY MEN ARE GOING TO SPLIT UP, SEARCH THE HOUSES A BIT, SPEED THIS PROCESS ALONG.
WHILE THEY'RE AT IT, I JUST WANT TO POINT OUT THAT WE'RE NOT TAKING A *SCRAP* OF YOUR FOOD. IT'S SLIM PICKENS IN THERE...
...AND I CAN'T BE THE ONLY ONE TO NOTICE YOU'VE GOT THE FAT LADY IN CHARGE OF KEEPING TRACK OF RATIONS, CAN I?
REGARDLESS, IF YOU GUYS STARVE TO DEATH, I DON'T GET SHIT. SO FOR NOW, YOUR FOOD STAYS WITH YOU.

WHAT DO YOU WANT ME TO SAY?

HOW ABOUT A FUCKING *THANK YOU?* YOU THINK THAT MIGHT BE IN ORDER?
LISTEN, PRICK. I KNOW WE STARTED OFF ON THE WRONG FOOT, I DIDN'T WANT TO KILL YOUR FRIEND... YOU FORCED MY FUCKING HAND.

I'M ACTUALLY *QUITE* REASONABLE IF YOU JUST FUCKING COOPERATE.
I'LL BELIEVE IT WHEN I SEE IT.

YOU SHOULD ALL GO HOME...

...BEFORE YOU LEARN JUST HOW *DANGEROUS* WE ALL ARE.

PARDON ME, YOUNG MAN, AND FUCKING EXCUSE THE SHIT OUT OF MY GODDAMN FRENCH... BUT DID YOU JUST THREATEN ME?
THAT SOUNDED LIKE A THREAT, BUT I LIKE TO BE DAMN SURE WHEN IT COMES TO THESE KINDS OF THINGS.

CARL. GO BACK TO THE HOUSE.
NOW.

I'M IN THE MIDDLE OF A FUCKING CONVERSATION HERE.
DON'T BE RUDE.

NOW, BOY... WHERE WERE WE? OH, YEAH... YOUR GIANT FUCKING MAN-SIZED BALLS.
I MIGHT NOT HAVE HEARD YOU CLEARLY. WHAT WERE YOU SAYING AGAIN?

THAT'S BETTER.
NOW LISTEN TO YOUR DADDY AND RUN THE FUCK ALONG.

CUTE KID.

I DON'T LIKE THIS.
I CAN SEE THAT.

RICK, HURRY!

WHAT IS IT?!
DENISE! SHE'S--

YOU SAID HALF, GODDAMN IT!
GIVE IT BACK!

PLEASE DON'T MISUNDERSTAND MY ASSOCIATE, MA'AM. I ASSURE YOU IF YOU REFERENCE YOUR ACCOUNTING OF WHAT DRUGS YOU HAD ON HAND **BEFORE** OUR ARRIVAL, YOU'LL FIND THAT MORE THAN HALF REMAINS.

ALL THE ASPIRIN, ALL THE PENICILLIN, ALL THE COLD MEDICINE--BUT ANYTHING SERIOUS, MORPHINE, OXYCONTIN, ANYTHING WE MIGHT NEED, ANYTHING THAT CAN BE **ABUSED**--
--HE'S TAKEN **ALL** THAT.

THE FACT REMAINS, HE'S TAKEN LESS THAN **HALF** OF YOUR MEDICINE STOCKPILES.

NOT **YET** HE HASN'T!
DENISE!

PUT THE GUN **DOWN!**

RICK?

YOU CAN'T LET THEM DO THIS. IF SOMETHING SERIOUS HAPPENS, LIKE WHAT HAPPENED TO CARL... I WON'T BE ABLE TO DO ANYTHING.
WE NEED THIS STUFF.

NEGAN, LISTEN...

STOP RIGHT THERE. YOUR BIG WALLS ARE ALL THE MEDICINE YOU NEED. DEAL'S A DEAL. WE'RE TAKING HALF.
UNLESS YOU WANT MY MEN TO DO ANOTHER PASS, PICK OUT SOME SOFT GOODS?

NO, IT'S OKAY.
TAKE IT.

WELL, THEN... I GUESS WE'LL BE GOING.
THANKS SO MUCH FOR YOUR TIME.

SEE YOU LATERS, ALLIGATORS.

OH, WAIT.

HOW CARELESS OF ME.

YOU DIDN'T THINK I'D LEAVE LUCILLE, DID YOU?
AND AFTER WHAT SHE DID... WHY WOULD YOU WANT HER?

THANKS FOR BEING SO ACCOMMODATING, FRIEND.

IN CASE YOU HAVEN'T CAUGHT ON...
...I JUST SLID MY DICK DOWN YOUR THROAT...
...AND YOU THANKED ME FOR IT.

AND WITH THAT, WE'LL BE GOING NOW...

TAKE YOUR TIME CLOSING THE GATE WHEN WE'RE GONE... ENJOY HOW SAFE WE MADE THIS AREA FOR YOU WHILE WE WERE WAITING.
WE'RE REALLY NICE PEOPLE WHEN YOU GET TO KNOW US.
HONEST.

HELP ME SHUT THE GATE.

WAIT, WHAT DID HE JUST SAY TO YOU WHEN HE WHISPERED?
IT'S NOT IMPORTANT.

RICK! NOT IMPORTANT?
THAT MAN IS DANGEROUS. I THINK EVERYTHING HE SAYS IS IMPORTANT.

THIS ISN'T.

IS THIS A JOKE TO YOU?! WHAT THE HELL ARE YOU DOING, RICK?
WHAT IS THIS?!

LET ME PUT THIS TO YOU AS CLEARLY AS I CAN.
I'M NOT IN CHARGE ANYMORE. NEGAN IS.

THAT IS HOW WE'RE GOING TO SURVIVE... BY FOLLOWING *HIS* RULES.
IF YOU DON'T WANT TO FOLLOW HIS RULES, THAT'S *FINE.* I'LL PULL THIS GATE BACK OPEN AND YOU CAN HIT THE ROAD.
SEE HOW YOU FARE OUT THERE ON YOUR OWN....

RICK. DON'T.

NO, THIS IS GODDAMN SERIOUS, AND I'M NOT GOING TO HAVE SOMEONE FLYING OFF THE HANDLE AND GETTING US ALL KILLED!
NO FUCKING WAY!

ANYONE WANT TO TRY THEIR LUCK? JUST SAY THE WORD AND I'LL OPEN THE GATE.
ANYONE?

THAT'S WHAT I THOUGHT.
WE NEED A NEW SUPPLY INVENTORY, WHAT WE HAVE, WHAT WE NEED, SO WE CAN GO GET IT... TO BE *MORE* THAN WELL-STOCKED WHEN THEY COME BACK.
THERE'S A LOT OF WORK TO BE DONE HERE.

GET TO IT.

CARL, GET DOWN HERE!
WE NEED TO TALK.

GOD DAMN IT, DWIGHT. PUT THAT THING AWAY.
THE HELL YOU DOING OUT HERE?! WE HEARD YOU WERE DEAD.

I WAS IN DEEP SHIT WHEN ALL YOU COWARDS FUCKING TUCKED TAIL AND RAN-- BUT I GOT OUT.
FIGURED THIS OUTPOST WAS THE CLOSEST, EVEN THOUGH IT WAS OUT OF MY WAY. FASTER TO GET A CAR FROM YOU AND TAKE IT BACK TO SANCTUARY.

THAT'S ALL WELL AND GOOD... BUT HOW LONG HAVE YOU BEEN *FOLLOWED?*

WHAT?!

SPOTTED YOU ALMOST A MILE DOWN THE ROAD... ALONG WITH YOUR ADMIRER.
HE'S HANGING BACK A WAYS. WHY YOU THINK WE DIDN'T JUST WAIT FOR YOU TO GET TO THE TOWER?

YOU GUYS GOT HIM? YOU COMING OVER?

JOHN? COME IN.

WE GOT NO INTENTION OF KILLING YOU--UNLESS YOU MAKE US.
I RECOGNIZE YOU FROM THE HILLTOP. REMEMBER YOU BEING KIND ENOUGH. SURRENDER, AND WE WON'T EVEN HURT YOU.

LIE FACE DOWN ON THE GROUND AND PUT YOUR HANDS BEHIND YOUR HEAD, OR WE'LL CUT YOUR BALLS OFF!

KRAK!
WHUMP!
THE FUCK--?!
WRAMM!

WROK!

DUMB ASS...

...GONNA DIE NOW.

PUT THE KNIFE AWAY, TARA.
RESTRAIN THAT SON OF A BITCH. HE'S MORE USE TO US ALIVE.

I THOUGHT OUR NEW FRIENDS WERE PLAYING BY THE RULES, FALLING IN LINE... SEEMS I WAS WRONG.
THEY CLEARLY SENT YOU TO FOLLOW ME BACK, SO THAT YOU WOULD KNOW WHERE WE LIVE... WHY WOULD YOU WANT TO KNOW THAT UNLESS YOU EVENTUALLY PLANNED ON PAYING US A VISIT?
NEGAN'S GOING TO HAVE A LOT OF QUESTIONS FOR YOU.

HOME SWEET HOME...

MIGHT WANT TO KEEP YOUR ARMS INSIDE THE JEEP...

GOD DAMN IT!

WHERE THE HELL DID HE--

NOT ONE WORD TO NEGAN ABOUT ANY OF THIS. NOT ONE DAMN WORD.
AGREED.

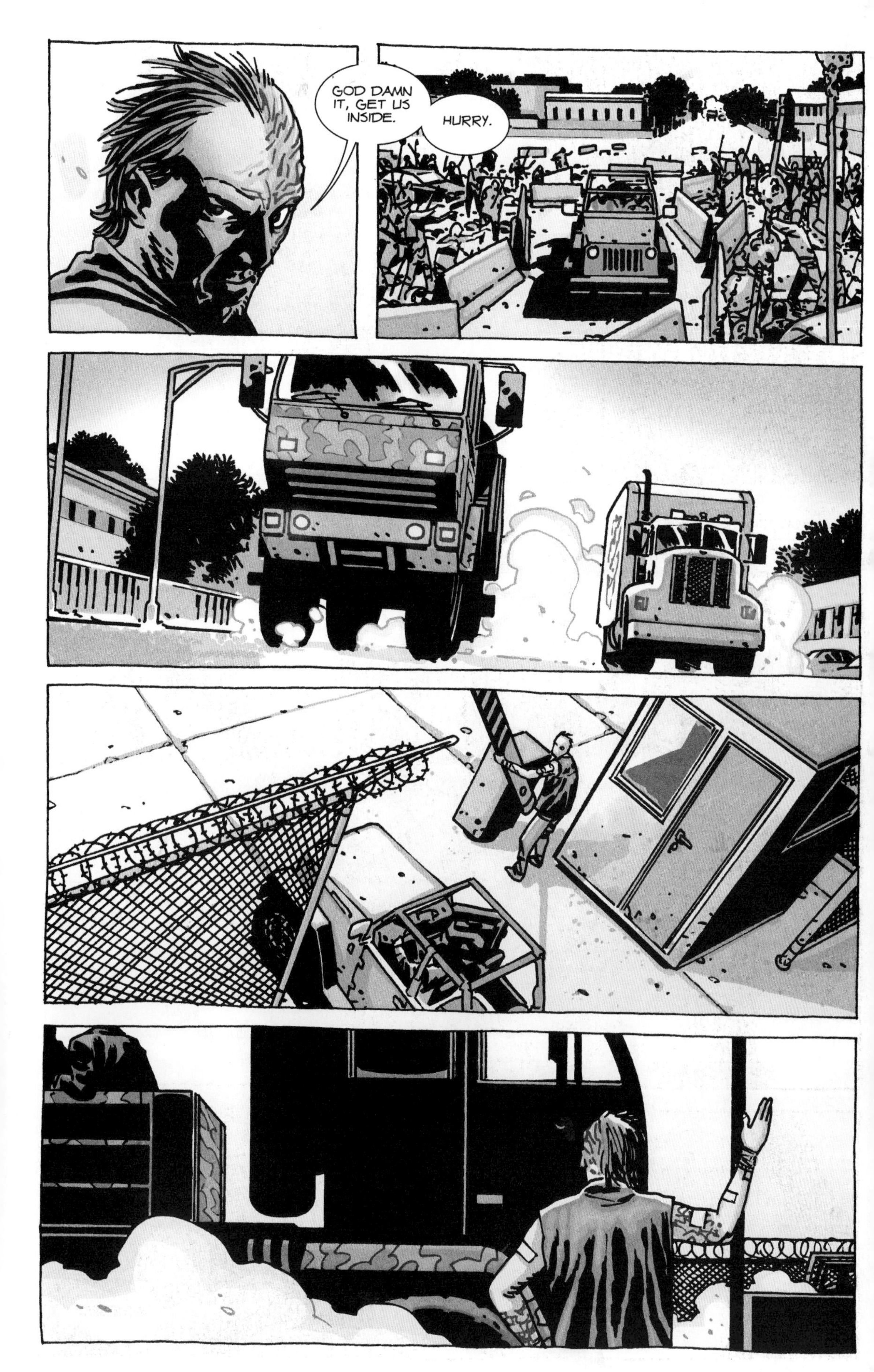
GOD DAMN IT, GET US INSIDE.
HURRY.

FIRST UNDEAD GHOULS, AND NOW WE GOTTA DEAL WITH MOTHER FUCKING *GHOSTS?*

REPORTS OF MY DEMISE WERE GREATLY EXAGGERATED.

THERE'S ALWAYS A NEXT TIME, I SUPPOSE.

OKAY, BOYS, LET'S GET THIS SHIT UNLOADED AND INSIDE.
GONNA BE DARK SOON, AND I WANT TO BE TUCKED IN AND CATCHING SOME Zs WITH AMPLE TIME TO THROW THE WOOD IN *AT LEAST* A COUPLE OF WIVES.
YOU KNOW WHAT I'M SAYING? I'M SAYING I'M GOING TO FUCK SOME OF MY GIRLS TONIGHT. GET IT?

THINK WE'LL GET ONE OF THESE MATTRESSES?
I FUCKING HOPE SO, BUT WHO KNOWS WHAT WE'LL HAVE TO DO TO EARN ONE.

THE HELL--?!

BRAKKA! BRAKKA! BRAKKA!

WHUDD!

STAY BACK!

WHAT THE FUCKING FUCK?!

I ONLY WANT NEGAN. HE KILLED MY FRIEND.
TURN HIM OVER TO ME, AND I'LL LET THE REST OF YOU LIVE. I'VE SEEN THE WEAPONS YOU USE, I KNOW YOU DON'T HAVE A LOT OF GUNS.
NO ONE ELSE NEEDS TO DIE.

GOD DAMN YOU'RE ADORABLE.
DID YOU PICK THAT GUN BECAUSE IT LOOKS COOL? YOU TOTALLY FUCKING DID, DIDN'T YOU?
IT'S ALMOST TWICE YOUR SIZE!

KID, I'M NOT GOING TO LIE TO YOU-- YOU SCARE THE FUCKING SHIT OUT OF ME.

BRAKKA! BRAKKA! BRAKKA! BRAKKA!

BRAKKA!
BRAKKA!

BRAKKA! BRAKKA! BRAKKA!

BRAKKA! BRAK--!

YOU LITTLE FUCK!

--KILL YOU!
KRAK!

DWIGHT!
BACK THE FUCK OFF!!

YOU'RE GOING TO BEAT ON A LITTLE DEFENSELESS CHILD?

IS THAT ANY WAY TO TREAT OUR NEW GUEST?

COME ON, I'LL SHOW YOU AROUND.

NEW PLAN, GUYS.
BURN THE DEAD. WE'LL UNLOAD THE TRUCK TOMORROW.

I DON'T THINK I'LL GET AROUND TO FUCKING SO MUCH AS ONE OF MY WIVES TONIGHT.

WHAT ARE YOU GOING TO DO TO ME?

NUMBER ONE, DON'T SHATTER MY IMAGE OF YOU. YOU'RE A FUCKING BADASS. YOU'RE NOT SCARED OF SHIT. DON'T BE SCARED OF ME. IT'S A DISAPPOINTMENT.
NUMBER TWO, DO YOU REALLY EXPECT ME TO RUIN THE SURPRISE? FUCK YOU, KID.

SERIOUSLY. FUCK YOU.
KNOCK! KNOCK!

WELCOME BACK, NEGAN. ALL THAT GUNFIRE-- SOMETHING TO BE CONCERNED ABOUT?
I'M HANDLING IT. IGNORE IT.

FAIR ENOUGH. UH... MOLLY STILL HAS THE COUGH. WHAT KIND OF MEDICINE YOU GET ON THIS RUN?

ALL KINDS OF GOOD SHIT. WE'LL CATALOGUE IT TOMORROW. I THINK YOU'VE GOT ENOUGH POINTS TO HAVE YOUR PICK.

THANK YOU, NEGAN.

WELCOME HOME, SIR. I SAW THE TRUCKS FROM THE WINDOWS ON LEVEL FIVE-- I HAD TO SEE YOU RIGHT AWAY.
THERE'S BEEN A SITUATION... BUT FIRST, IS THAT GUNFIRE SOMETHING TO BE CONCERNED ABOUT?

NOT ANYMORE. LEAD THE WAY, CARSON.

THIS DOESN'T HAVE TO DO WITH AMBER, DOES IT?
I'M AFRAID IT DOES.
FUCKING SHIT, IS THAT A DISAPPOINTMENT. I WANT TO TALK TO HER FIRST.

FIND MARK, BUT DON'T DO ANYTHING. JUST KEEP TABS ON HIM.

YES, SIR.

NEGAN HAS RETURNED!

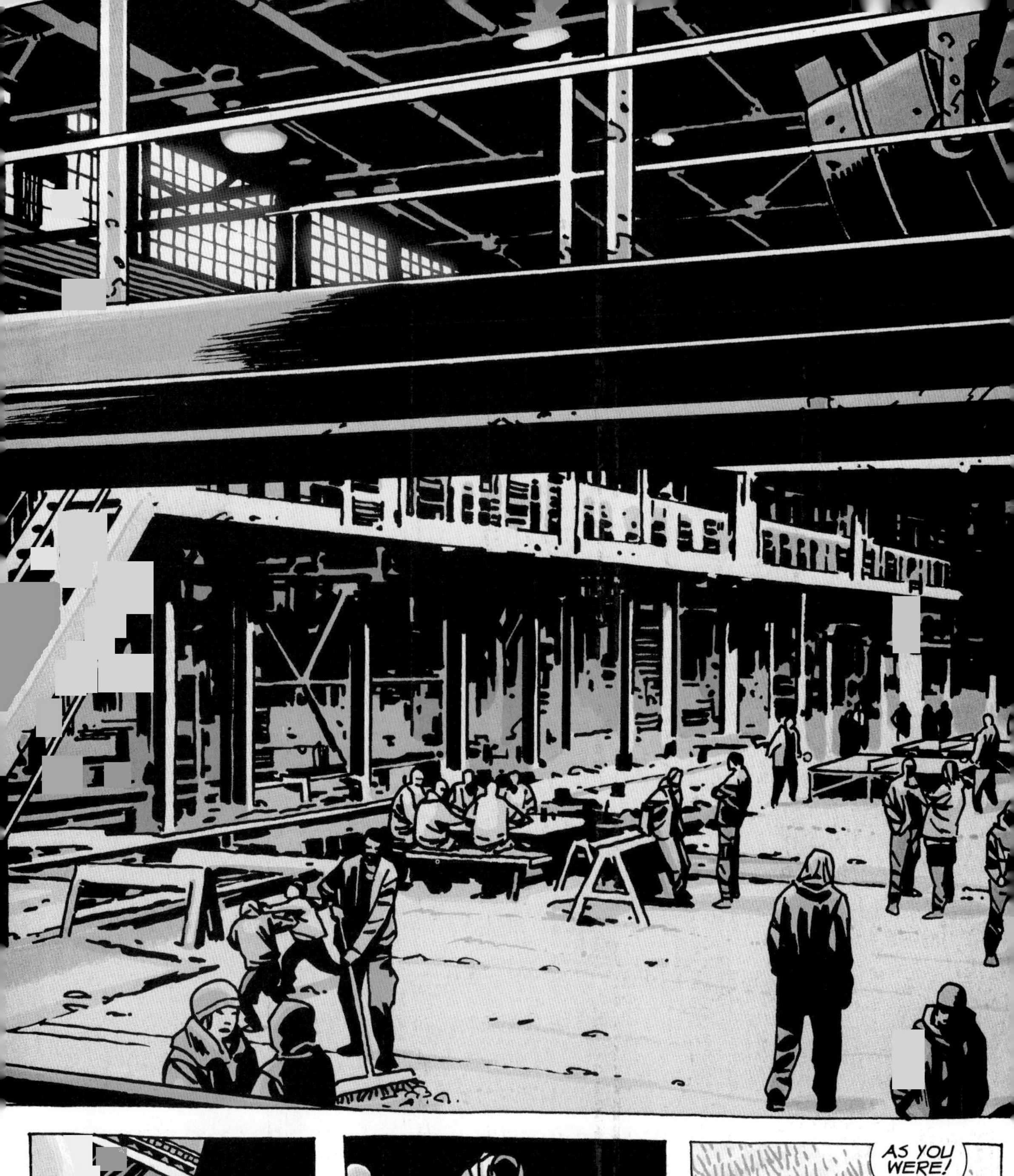

AS YOU WERE!
SEE THAT, BOY?
RESPECT.

GOD FUCKING DAMN IT, AMBER...
SHE KNOWS SHE FUCKED UP, NEGAN. GO EASY ON HER.
I EVER HIT **ANY** OF YOU? CALM THE FUCK DOWN.

I KNOW, RIGHT? EVERY WOMAN WHERE YOU'RE FROM DRESSES LIKE AN ELDERLY LESBIAN.
YOU'RE GOING TO WANT TO STARE AT THEIR TITTIES. I WON'T MIND, ***THEY*** WON'T MIND. KNOCK YOURSELF THE FUCK OUT.

NOW, WHERE WERE WE?
SHE JUST MADE A ***MISTAKE,*** OKAY? YOU KNOW THE TRANSITION ISN'T EASY FOR US--

SHERRY, WILL YOU PLEASE STEP THE FUCK ASIDE SO I CAN TALK TO AMBER?

AMBER, HONEY. YOU DON'T HAVE TO BE SCARED. YOUR POSITION HERE IS COMPLETELY VOLUNTARY. I DON'T WANT ANYONE HERE IF THEY DON'T WANT TO BE.
YOU UNDERSTAND THAT, RIGHT?
UH-HUH.
SO YOU KNOW THAT IF YOU WANT TO LEAVE, AND GO BACK TO MARK AND BE WITH HIM--YOU'LL FORFEIT YOUR PRIVILEGES AND GO BACK TO WHATEVER JOB YOU HAD BEFORE SHERRY BROUGHT YOU TO US, BUT YOU CAN.
OF COURSE YOU CAN... BUT AMBER... WHAT CAN'T YOU DO?

CHEAT ON YOU.

EXACTLY FUCKING RIGHT!
YOU CAN'T FUCKING CHEAT ON ME, AMBER!

I'M SURE YOU'VE HAD PLENTY OF TIME TO THINK ABOUT THIS. SO WHAT'S IT GOING TO BE? YOU GOING BACK TO MARK? BACK TO EARNING POINTS? WORKING FOR YOUR SUPPER?
OR ARE YOU STAYING?

STAYING...
I LOVE YOU, NEGAN.

OF COURSE YOU DO. YOU KNOW WHAT HAS TO HAPPEN NOW? IF YOU'RE STAYING?
Y-- YES...

OKAY THEN. SHERRY, FIND CARSON... TELL HIM TO PREPARE THE IRON.

CLOSE THE DOOR.

ARE THEY ALL YOUR--

WIVES? YEAH. I ALWAYS WANTED TO BE ABLE TO FUCK A WHOLE BUNCH OF WOMEN--SO WHY SETTLE DOWN WITH JUST ONE? I SEE NO REASON TO FOLLOW THE OLD BORING RULES.
LET'S MAKE LIFE BETTER. WHY NOT?

WAIT, YOU KNOW WHAT FUCKING IS, RIGHT?

YEAH.
KIND OF.
SEX STUFF.

NOT GOING THERE. NO FUCKING WAY.
LET'S GET STARTED.

STARTED ON WHAT?

I'D LIKE TO GET TO KNOW YOU A LITTLE BETTER, CARL.
FIRST, I WANT TO TELL YOU HOW MOTHERFUCKING **SMART** YOU ARE, JUST IN CASE YOU DON'T ALREADY KNOW. YOU'RE WHAT, **TWELVE?** WHO CARES?
I'D EXPECT A KID YOUR AGE TO BE RUNNING AWAY, TRYING TO GET OUT--HAVING MY PEOPLE CHASE YOU ALL OVER THIS MILL. BUT YOU STAYED RIGHT WITH ME. I BARELY EVEN HAD TO LOOK AT YOU.
BECAUSE YOU **KNEW** THAT IF YOU FUCKED SOMETHING ELSE UP, I'D CHASE YOU DOWN AND BREAK YOUR LITTLE KID NECK. RIGHT?

I--
DOESN'T MATTER.

YOU KILLED LIKE FIVE OR SIX OF MY MEN JUST NOW--SO MANY I DIDN'T EVEN GET A GOOD FUCKING COUNT.
THIS CAN'T GO UNPUNISHED, SO--

YOU KNOW WHAT, **STOP.** I CAN'T GO ON LIKE THIS. IT'S LIKE TALKING TO A FUCKING BIRTHDAY PRESENT.
TAKE THAT SHIT OFF YOUR FACE--I GOTTA SEE WHAT GRANDMA GOT ME.

NO.

SIX MEN. PUNISHMENT.
REALLY WANT TO PISS ME OFF?

THAT'S BETTER.

ALMOST THERE...

FUCKING CHRIST, MAN! NO WONDER YOU COVER THAT SHIT UP. YOU LOOK **DISGUSTING.** HAVE YOU **SEEN** IT?!
I MEAN-- HAVE YOU LOOKED IN A MIRROR? I WOULDN'T BLAME YOU IF YOU HADN'T. IT'S FUCKING **GROSS.**
I CAN SEE YOUR FUCKING EYE SOCKET-- YOUR GODDAMN SKULL IS EXPOSED.
NOW I WANT TO TOUCH IT. CAN I TOUCH IT?

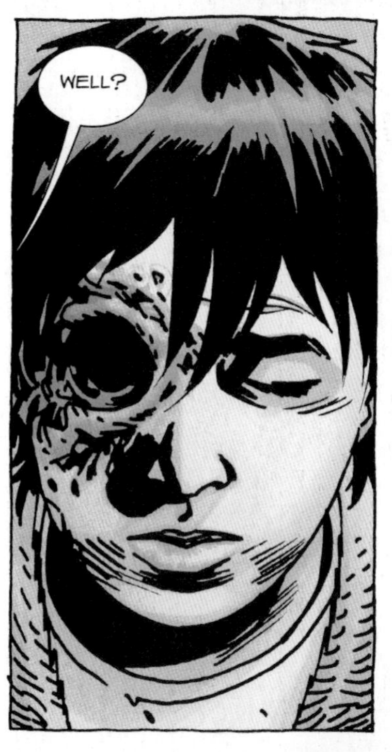
WELL?

OH, DAMN. LOOK...
HOLY SHIT, KID. I'M SORRY.
I DIDN'T MEAN TO...

IT'S EASY TO FORGET YOU'RE JUST A KID. I WASN'T TRYING TO HURT YOUR FEELINGS OR ANYTHING.
THIS ISN'T WHAT I--

I'M SORRY TO INTERRUPT, NEGAN.
YOU LEFT LUCILLE IN THE TRUCK, AND I KNOW HOW YOU DON'T LIKE TO BE WITHOUT HER...

NO SHIT? I NEVER DO THAT.
I GUESS A KID FIRING A MACHINE GUN IS A HELL OF A DISTRACTION.

ALL JOKING ASIDE, YOU LOOK RAD AS FUCK. I WOULDN'T COVER THAT SHIT UP.
WON'T BE A HIT WITH THE LADIES, BUT WON'T ANYONE FUCK WITH YOU LOOKING LIKE THAT. NO, SIR.

YOU CARRIED HER ALL THE WAY UP HERE FOR ME?
YES, SIR.
WERE YOU GENTLE? WERE YOU KIND?
UH...

DID YOU TREAT HER LIKE A LADY?

UM... YES.

DID YOU EAT HER PUSSY LIKE A LADY?

WELL, I... UH...

I'M JUST FUCKING WITH YOU! A BASEBALL BAT DOESN'T HAVE A PUSSY!

NOW GET THE FUCK OUT OF HERE.

ALL PLEASANTRIES ASIDE, AND I THINK YOU'D AGREE I'VE BEEN MORE THAN FUCKING PLEASANT SINCE I FOUND YOU HERE...
...YOU KILLED A BUNCH OF MY MEN WITH A FUCKING MACHINE GUN. FUCKING MOWED THEM DOWN.
I NEED SOMETHING IN RETURN FOR THAT. PLAIN AND SIMPLE.

SING ME A SONG.

WHAT?
I CAN'T... I DON'T KNOW ANY.

FUCKING BULLSHIT YOU DON'T KNOW ANY SONGS. YOU NEVER WENT TO CAMP? MOM DIDN'T SING TO YOU? NEVER DROVE WITH DAD LISTENING TO THE CLASSIC ROCK STATION?
YOU KILLED MY MEN, AND YOU'RE GOING TO SING ME A FUCKING SONG.

OKAY.

YOU--
AHEM!
...

YOU ARE MY SUNSHINE...
GO ON.
...MY ONLY SUNSHINE. YOU MAKE ME HAPPY...

...WHEN SKIES ARE GRAY.

YOU'LL NEVER KNOW DEAR...

...HOW MUCH I LOVE YOU.

DON'T LET ME DISTRACT YOU, KID.
CONTINUE.

SO...
SO PLEASE DON'T...

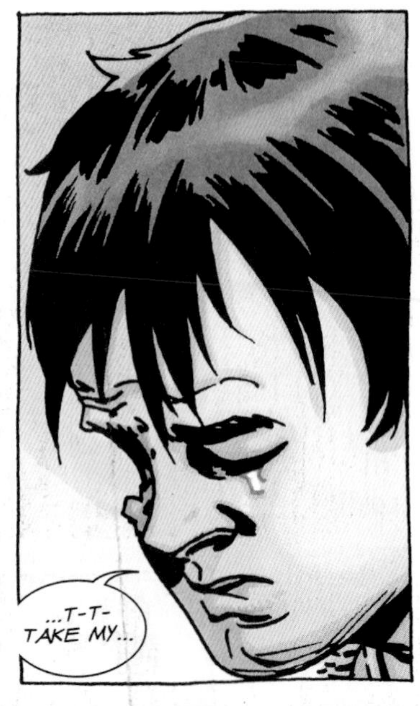
...T-T-TAKE MY...

...SUNSHINE...

...AWAY.

THAT WAS PRETTY FUCKING GOOD.
LUCILLE LOVES BEING SUNG TO.
IT'S ABOUT THE ONLY THING SHE LIKES MORE THAN BASHING IN BRAINS. WEIRD, HUH?

YOUR MOTHER SING YOU THAT SONG?
WHERE'S SHE AT NOW?

YEAH.
DEAD.

KNOCK. KNOCK.
HOLD THAT THOUGHT.

THE *IRON* IS READY, SIR.
AWESOME.
GATHER EVERYONE. WE'LL BE DOWN IN A MINUTE.

WE'RE ALL HERE, NEGAN. WE'RE READY TO BEGIN.

AIN'T THAT GRAND.
HOLD THIS FOR ME.
WHAT YOU ARE ALL ABOUT TO WITNESS IS GOING TO BE UNPLEASANT. IT DOESN'T HAVE TO BE, IT DOESN'T EVEN HAVE TO HAPPEN.
FUCKING HELL I WISH IT WOULDN'T. I WISH I COULD JUST LET THIS SLIDE... IGNORE THE RULES...
...BUT I CAN'T.
WHY?

THE RULES KEEP US ALIVE.
THANKS.
THAT'S RIGHT. WE SURVIVE, WE PROVIDE SECURITY FOR OTHERS, WE BRING CIVILIZATION BACK TO THIS WORLD-- WE'RE THE SAVIORS.

AND WE CAN'T DO THAT WITHOUT RULES. THE RULES ARE WHAT MAKES EVERYTHING WORK.

NO MATTER HOW SMALL, OR INSIGNIFICANT, THE RULES ARE TO BE FOLLOWED.
I KNOW IT MAY SEEM TRIVIAL, OR EVEN CALLOUS ON MY PART. THERE'S NO FUCKING TRUTH TO THAT AT ALL.

WHEN I CHOOSE A NEW WIFE, THE PROCESS IS COMPLETELY VOLUNTARY. IT'S AN HONOR TO BE WITH ME, TO NO LONGER HAVE TO EARN POINTS TO TRADE FOR GOODS AND SERVICES.
BUT IT COMES WITH A PRICE... TOTAL DEVOTION... AND THAT CAN SOMETIMES BE A HARD PILL FOR OTHERS TO SWALLOW.
BUT SWALLOW IT THEY MUST...

OR IT'S THE IRON FOR YOU.

SORRY, MARK.
IT IS WHAT IT IS.

YEEAAAGH!!
SSSSSS

AAAGG--

SEE? ALL DONE.
NOW, WAS THAT SO BAD?

HUH? PASSED OUT?!
PUSSY.

THIS MATTER IS SETTLED. ALL IS FORGIVEN.
MARK WILL FOREVER BEAR THE SHAME OF HIS ACTIONS ON HIS FACE, ALL WILL KNOW WHAT HE'S DONE.

I HOPE THAT WE HAVE ALL LEARNED SOMETHING TODAY.

BECAUSE I REALLY DON'T FUCKING WANT TO DO THAT SHIT EVER AGAIN.

YOU SEE THAT?
PRETTY FUCKING CRAZY SHIT, HUH?
YOU PROBABLY THINK I'M A LUNATIC.
NOW LET'S FIGURE OUT WHAT TO DO WITH YOU.

MARK?

I'M SO SORRY-- I--

DON'T.

SOMEONE WILL SEE, AND THEY WON'T HESITATE TO SELL YOU OUT.
YOU'LL ONLY MAKE THINGS *WORSE.* LET HIM GO.

COME ON, AMBER.
DWIGHT, I...

SHUT UP, BITCH.

CAN I... WRAP UP MY FACE?

NO, YOU ABSOLUTELY FUCKING CANNOT.

WHY *THE FUCK* NOT?

WHOA-HO-HO!
LOOK AT THIS BAD MOTHER FUCKER!
NICE.

YOU CAN'T, BECAUSE I'M NOT *DONE* WITH YOU.
YOU DIDN'T REALLY THINK I'D LET YOU OFF FOR A *SONG*, DID YOU?

...

YOU'RE A SMART KID. WHAT DO YOU THINK I SHOULD DO? YOU KNOW I CAN'T JUST LET YOU GO... SHOULD I JUST KILL YOU? IRON YOUR FACE?
YOU HAVE ANY SUGGESTIONS FOR ME?

I THINK YOU SHOULD JUMP OUT A WINDOW TO SAVE ME THE TROUBLE OF KILLING YOU.

HA! HA! HA! HA! HA! HA!

HEH.
THERE'S THE BOY THAT IMPRESSED THE HELL OUT OF ME. NICE ONE. REALLY FUCKING NICE.
HEH... HOO BOY...

TRUTH IS, I LOOK AT YOU... AND I HAVE A REALLY HARD TIME THINKING OF ANY PUNISHMENT THAT WOULD BE WORSE THAN WHAT YOU'VE ALREADY ENDURED...

BUT I'LL THINK OF SOMETHING.

KRAKK!

KRUKK!

VROOM!
FINALLY!

THERE'S TOO MANY OF THEM!
WE HAVE TO TURN BACK!
NO, GOD DAMN IT!
NOT YET!

BLAM!
I'M NOT GIVING UP!
WHUMP!

WE CAN HANDLE THIS!
BLAM!
MICHONNE!
WHUDD!

GOT IT.
SVAASH!

BLAM!
FUCK!
FUCK!

NICHOLAS-- DUCK!
KA-POW!

SLAKK!
BLAM!

BLAM!

BLAM! BLAM!

BLAM! BLAM!

CLICK. CLICK.

WE'LL TRY AGAIN TOMORROW.
WE'RE NOT GIVING UP.

WHAT ARE THEY EVEN DOING OUT THERE? THEY DON'T EVEN KNOW WHAT DIRECTION TO LOOK IN.
IT'S HIS SON. YOU EXPECT HIM TO JUST SIT HERE AND HOPE CARL COMES BACK?

I'D LIKE TO KNOW THE SAFETY OF THIS COMMUNITY ISN'T DEPENDENT ON THE BEHAVIOR OF THAT BOY.
YOU THINK WE CAN AFFORD A DISTRACTION LIKE THIS NOW?

SPENCER--I THINK I'VE SAID MAYBE TWO WORDS TO THE GUY, BUT HE SEEMS LIKE HE'S GOT OUR BEST INTERESTS IN MIND. I THINK THE GOOD LORD HIMSELF BROUGHT RICK HERE TO PROTECT US.
AND I THINK YOU GOT A LOT MORE CRITICAL OF RICK GRIMES ONCE HE STOLE YOUR GIRLFRIEND.

SHE WAS NEVER MY GIRLFRIEND, ERIN.
WHICH MAKES IT THAT MUCH MORE PAINFUL, I'M SURE.
YOU'RE A GOOD MAN, SPENCER...

...DON'T LET THIS DRIVE YOU CRAZY.
BOYS! IT'S GETTING DARK... LET'S HEAD HOME!

WHAT ARE YOU SAYING, EXACTLY?
I'M SAYING WE MIGHT BE BETTER OFF OUT THERE, ON THE ROAD, ON OUR OWN.
THESE SAVIORS... THIS GUY NEGAN... HAVE YOU BEEN PAYING ATTENTION? WHAT HAPPENS WHEN SUPPLIES AREN'T ENOUGH? WHAT IF HE WANTS TO MOVE IN HERE?
AND RICK IS WORKING *WITH* HIM? COOPERATING?

RICK IS SPENDING EVERY WAKING HOUR TRYING TO FIND HIS SON--AND WE'RE HELPING HIM KEEP THIS COMMUNITY TOGETHER WHILE HE DOES IT.
AND DAMN IT, ERIC, WE *OWE* HIM THAT.
WE'RE *NOT* LEAVING.

I'M NOT SAYING PACK UP AND GO TONIGHT. I'M SAYING WE SHOULD THINK ABOUT IT-- *PREPARE* FOR IT.
WE MAY NOT HAVE A *CHOICE.*

ARE YOU SAYING PREPARE FOR AN ASSAULT? PREPARE TO RUN?
RUN WHERE, ERIC?!
HAVE YOU FORGOTTEN WHAT IT WAS LIKE OUT THERE? YOU WERE *STABBED* LAST TIME WE WENT OUT.

WE DID OKAY ON OUR OWN OUT THERE, RECRUITING PEOPLE. WE KNOW HOW TO SURVIVE.
AND I GOT STABBED SEEKING PEOPLE OUT-- TRYING TO BRING THEM BACK *HERE.* WE WOULDN'T BE DOING THAT.

I'M SORRY, BUT I THINK BEING OUT THERE, SLEEPING IN ABANDONED CARS, FEARING FOR OUR LIVES... IT WAS A FUN ADVENTURE, AND IT WAS EXCITING. YEAH.
--BUT I THINK IT WAS ONLY BEARABLE BECAUSE I KNEW WE WERE ALWAYS COMING BACK *HERE.*

THIS PLACE IS SPECIAL. YOU KNOW THAT. RICK KNOWS THAT... WE ALL KNOW THAT. WE SHOULDN'T BE TALKING ABOUT ESCAPE PLANS OR ABANDONING THIS PLACE.
WE SHOULD BE TALKING ABOUT SECURING THIS PLACE, MAKING IT WORK. WE SHOULD BE GOING OUT ON RUNS FOR FERTILIZER, SEEDS, WHATEVER WE NEED TO GROW CROPS, PRODUCE FOOD TO TRADE WITH THE SAVIORS.
WE NEED TO WORK TO MAKE THIS SITUATION SMOOTHER.

YOU REALLY BELIEVE GIVING THIS GUY HALF OF OUR SUPPLIES IS A FAIR TAX WE SHOULD LIVE WITH?
YOU'VE LOST YOUR FUCKING MIND, AARON.

HEY, CALM DOWN. I DON'T THINK IT'S FAIR, I JUST RECOGNIZE WE'RE NOT IN A POSITION TO FIGHT BACK.
WE START PROVIDING THEM WITH MORE THAN THEY CAN HANDLE-- THINGS START GETTING A LOT LESS TENSE. WE CAN TRADE GOODS WITH THE HILLTOP, TOO.

SOUNDS LIKE A PIPE DREAM.

NO, IT SOUNDS LIKE CIVILIZATION.
I THINK THAT'S WHY RICK IS WORKING WITH THIS GUY. THIS COULD CHANGE EVERYTHING.

ANSWER ME THIS. YOU FEEL SAFE HERE? NOW, AFTER ALL THIS?

ONLY PLACE I FEEL SAFE IS IN YOUR ARMS.

OH, FUCK YOU-- COME HERE.

IT'S LATE. WAS WORRIED YOU GUYS WEREN'T MAKING IT BACK TONIGHT.
WE WERE FURTHER OUT THAN WE THOUGHT, STARTED BACK TOO LATE.

WE'LL GO BACK OUT FIRST THING IN THE MORNING.
LET'S JUST TRY TO GET SOME SLEEP.

RICK.
RICK, WAKE UP.

JESUS?
WHAT THE HELL?

SORRY TO STARTLE--
SHHH.
WAIT.

DIDN'T WANT TO WAKE YOU BUT I THOUGHT THIS NEWS WAS WORTH--

WRAMM!
HOW DID YOU GET IN HERE?!

HEATH LET ME IN THE GATE... AND YOU DIDN'T LOCK YOUR FRONT DOOR. I KNOCKED IF IT MAKES YOU FEEL ANY BETTER.
RICK... I FOUND NEGAN... I KNOW WHERE HE LIVES.

DID YOU SEE CARL?
NO. WHERE? IS HE IN HIS ROOM?

HE'S GONE. DISAPPEARED THE DAY NEGAN LEFT. I THINK NEGAN TOOK HIM, BUT I DON'T WANT TO RILE EVERYONE UP--MAKE IT HARDER TO KEEP THE PEACE... I'VE BEEN PLAYING DUMB...
...BEEN GOING OUT EVERY DAY LOOKING FOR HIM--WHEN WE'RE REALLY TRYING TO TRACK DOWN NEGAN AND THE SAVIORS. I JUST... COULDN'T WAIT FOR YOU TO COME BACK...

SAW HIS CARAVAN ENTER--THEY'VE GOT A WALL, CAN'T REALLY SEE INSIDE. AS I WAS STARTING BACK ON MY WAY HERE--I HEARD AUTOMATIC WEAPON FIRE... DON'T KNOW WHAT THAT WAS ABOUT.

ABRAHAM'S MACHINE GUN IS MISSING.

I CAN TAKE YOU THERE IN THE MORNING.

I CAN'T WAIT THAT LONG.

THEY'VE GOT *WHAT* AROUND THE WALL?
A KILLING FIELD... I DON'T KNOW WHAT ELSE YOU'D CALL IT. THEY'RE USING THE DEAD AS A DEFENSIVE MEASURE... PRETTY SMART.
THEY'VE GOT THEM IMPALED INTO THE GROUND, CHAINED TO CARS, TIED DOWN, SOME MORE MOBILE THAN OTHERS.
JUST GETTING TO THE WALL COULD BE A PROBLEM...

I KNOW A WAY.
ROAMERS WON'T EVEN NOTICE US.

AND ONCE WE'RE INSIDE--HOW DO WE FIND HIM? YOU SAID THIS PLACE HAS HOW MANY FLOORS?
I DON'T KNOW... A BUNCH. TEN? IT'S A HUGE PLACE.

THAT DOESN'T SOUND PROMISING.
THERE A PLACE NEARBY WHERE I COULD SET UP, WATCH THEM THROUGH MY SCOPE? IT'D BE BEST TO KNOW WHAT WE'RE RUNNING INTO-- MAYBE I'D SEE CARL.

SOME TALL TREES NEARBY--DON'T KNOW HOW CLEAR A VIEW YOU COULD GET WITHOUT RISK OF BEING SPOTTED.

I'M JUST GOING TO KNOCK.

WHAT?!

WATCH THE ROAD.
I'LL KNOCK AND ASK THEM TO GIVE HIM TO ME. NEGAN WANTS US SUBMISSIVE, WORKING FOR HIM-- HE'S NOT LOOKING TO GO TO WAR.

IT'LL BE ENOUGH OF A FUCK YOU TO SHOW HIM WE KNOW WHERE HE LIVES. HE MIGHT BE OFF BALANCE BECAUSE OF THAT. WILLING TO GIVE UP CARL TO NOT APPEAR THREATENING, TO KEEP US FROM ATTACKING HIM.
YOU THINK THAT'LL WORK?

PLACE THAT BIG--WE'RE GOING TO FIND HIM BEFORE THEY FIND US? NOT LIKELY.
SEEMS LIKE THIS COULD BE THE ONLY WAY. I DON'T KNOW. I'M STILL THINKING ABOUT IT.

I'VE BEEN DEALING WITH NEGAN A LOT LONGER THAN YOU--AND I CAN SAY HE'S COMPLETELY UNPREDICTABLE.
THIS COULD GO EITHER WAY.

GUYS.

I'LL HANDLE THIS. STAY PUT.

TO HELL WITH THAT.
JUST FOLLOW MY LEAD.

JUST THE MAN I WANTED TO SEE... HOW MOTHER FUCKING CONVENIENT IT IS TO MEET YOU ON THE ROAD LIKE THIS.
WHERE WERE YOU HEADED?

TO SEE YOU.
MY WORD, AND YOU WERE HEADED IN THE RIGHT DIRECTION. HOW *STRANGE.* WELL, IF I DIDN'T KNOW BETTER, I'D SUSPECT--

WHERE IS CARL?
WHO? OH, I'M KIDDING.
THAT'S ACTUALLY THE REASON I'M HERE... I WAS COMING TO SEE *YOU,* IF YOU CAN BELIEVE IT.

IT'S LIKE THE FUCKING GIFT OF THE MAGI HERE. DOES THAT APPLY? COMBS FOR HAIR AND ALL--I GUESS MAYBE IF WE'D PASSED EACH OTHER, THEN IT WOULD... WHERE WAS I?
OH, YEAH!

I CAN'T FUCKING WAIT UNTIL YOU SEE WHAT I'VE **DONE** TO YOUR LITTLE BOY!

WHUDD!

WRAMM!
WHAUGH!

THIS CRAZY FUCK--!
YOU'RE A DEAD MAN!

NO!
HE'S MINE!

WRAMM!
MY SON!

WHAT DID YOU DO TO MY SON?!

HUURK!
OFF ME--!

THINK I'M GOING TO LET SOME ONE-HANDED PIECE OF SHIT BEAT ME UP--IN FRONT OF MY OWN MEN?
HAVE YOU LOST YOUR FUCKING MIND?!

WELL?!
WROKK!

STAND THE FUCK UP, YOU FUCKING FUCKER. BEFORE I FUCK YOU UP EVEN MORE.

THAP.

NOW I'M SUPER FUCKING PISSED OFF.

YOU HAVE ***NO CLUE*** HOW MUCH YOU'RE GOING TO REGRET HAVING DONE THIS IN A COUPLE MINUTES.
GET THE BOY!

AAGH!

GOD FUCKING DAMN IT!

WROKK!

DID YOU FUCKING BITE ME?!
FOR FUCK'S SAKE, MAN!

STAND DOWN, WOMAN.
YOU'VE ALL GOTTEN THIS FAR WITHOUT BEING SLAUGHTERED-- DON'T PRESS YOUR LUCK.

LET'S ALL JUST TAKE A FUCKING BREATH AND TRY TO CALM THE FUCK DOWN.
FUCK...

MY SON...
MY SON...
DAD?!

I'M SO SORRY, DAD.

CARL...

POOR CHOICE OF WORDS, I'LL ADMIT.
WHAT I *SHOULD* HAVE SAID WAS...
I CAN'T FUCKING WAIT UNTIL YOU SEE THAT I'VE DONE *NOTHING* TO YOUR LITTLE BOY.
I'LL ADMIT I WAS TRYING TO INSTIGATE YOU... THAT'S ON ME. I DIDN'T THINK YOU'D FUCKING TAKE MY BAIT SO EASILY. I... YOU CAUGHT ME OFF GUARD.
SHIT.

I NEVER SHOULD HAVE SAID... I DIDN'T MEAN IT.
I'M SORRY.
IT'S OKAY, CARL. YOU'RE OKAY. THAT'S ALL THAT MATTERS.

I WAS STUPID. I WAS TRYING TO SHOW YOU I WAS GROWN UP, THAT I COULD DO STUFF...
...INSTEAD, I MESSED EVERYTHING UP.

I THOUGHT I'D NEVER SEE YOU AGAIN...

CAN I SAY SOMETHING?

I DON'T QUITE UNDERSTAND THE HOSTILITY IN THAT LOOK.
NO FUCKING SIR.

I GAVE YOU YOUR SON BACK... WITHOUT HARMING SO MUCH AS ONE EXPOSED BONE ON HIS HEAD.
HEH.
I SAID "EXPOSED BONE" INSTEAD OF "HAIR." THAT'S NOT EVEN GETTING A CHUCKLE?
WELL, I THOUGHT IT WAS FUNNY, YOU STOIC PIECE OF SHIT.

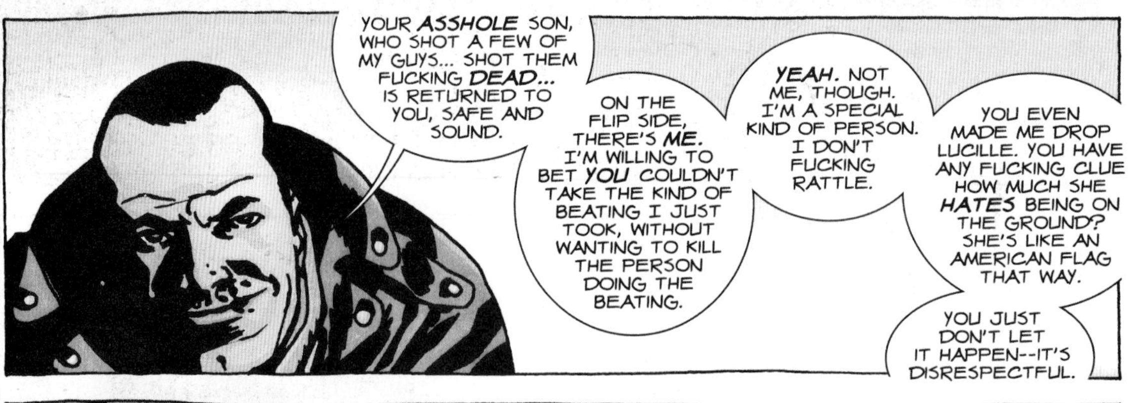
YOUR ASSHOLE SON, WHO SHOT A FEW OF MY GUYS... SHOT THEM FUCKING DEAD... IS RETURNED TO YOU, SAFE AND SOUND.
ON THE FLIP SIDE, THERE'S ME. I'M WILLING TO BET YOU COULDN'T TAKE THE KIND OF BEATING I JUST TOOK, WITHOUT WANTING TO KILL THE PERSON DOING THE BEATING.
YEAH. NOT ME, THOUGH. I'M A SPECIAL KIND OF PERSON. I DON'T FUCKING RATTLE.
YOU EVEN MADE ME DROP LUCILLE. YOU HAVE ANY FUCKING CLUE HOW MUCH SHE HATES BEING ON THE GROUND? SHE'S LIKE AN AMERICAN FLAG THAT WAY.
YOU JUST DON'T LET IT HAPPEN--IT'S DISRESPECTFUL.

STILL-- HERE I AM, FRIENDLY AS A FUCKLESS FUCK ON FREE FUCK DAY.

WHAT'S GOT YOU BEING SO NICE ALL OF A SUDDEN?

I'VE GOT A LOT TO MAKE UP FOR.

YOU THINK I'VE GOT ALL THESE LITTLE COMMUNITIES AT MY FEET BECAUSE I ROAM THE COUNTRYSIDE BASHING IN ASIAN-AMERICAN SKULLS?
THAT'S NO FUCKING WAY TO MAKE FRIENDS.
EVERYONE TOES THE LINE BECAUSE I PROVIDE THEM A SERVICE. I KEEP THEM SAFE. WE'RE THE SAVIORS, NOT THE KILL YOUR FRIENDS SO YOU DON'T FUCKING LIKE US AT ALLS.

ARE WE GOING TO KILL YOUR FRIENDS IF YOU DON'T COOPERATE?! ABSOLUTELY. I'M PRETTY SURE I'VE ESTABLISHED THAT.
AND NOW I'VE ESTABLISHED THAT IF YOU DO COOPERATE, AS I BELIEVE YOU ARE, WE WON'T DO BAD THINGS TO YOUR SON, EVEN THOUGH HE KILLED A FEW OF MY MEN BECAUSE HE DIDN'T FUCKING KNOW ANY BETTER.

YOU FOLLOWING THIS AT ALL?

I THINK SO.
YEAH.

THEN WHY YOU STILL GIVING ME THE STINK EYE?
AREN'T WE FUCKING FRIENDS?

I WILL COOPERATE. I'VE TOLD YOU THIS ALREADY.
BUT YOU DON'T STRIKE ME AS THE KIND OF GUY WHO'D WANT ME TO *LIE* AND SAY THAT WE'RE FRIENDS, OR BELIEVE ME IF I DID SAY THAT.

POINT TAKEN.

OKAY THEN. THIS FEELS LIKE PROGRESS TO ME. YEAH.
THIS WAS GOOD. I'M FEELING REALLY FUCKING GOOD HERE.

JUST SO I'M ABSOLUTELY CRYSTAL FUCKING CLEAR. THERE WAS A CLEAR MESSAGE I WANTED TO CONVEY HERE TODAY. THAT MESSAGE IS...
I CAN BE REASONABLE.
I CAN BE COMPLETELY FUCKING REASONABLE.

IN FACT... I FUCKING PREFER IT THAT WAY.
I DON'T WANT TO DO THE BAD THINGS I DO. I ONLY DO THEM TO SET BOUNDARIES, TO MAKE PEOPLE AWARE OF THE CONSEQUENCES OF THEIR ACTIONS.

I TAKE NO JOY IN THOSE DEEDS.
LUCILLE ON THE OTHER HAND...
THANKFULLY, SHE'S NOT IN CHARGE.

SO ARE WE GOOD HERE?
GOOD.
WE'LL BE MAKING ANOTHER SUPPLY RUN SOON. WE'LL SEE YOU THEN.

THAT ALL COMPLETE FUCKING BULLSHIT?

ACTUALLY, NO... HE'S GOT WEIRD ASS RULES, BUT IF YOU FOLLOW THEM, HE DOES SEEM TO BE PRETTY REASONABLE. MOST OF THE TIME.

STILL SOME TIME BEFORE DARK. WE SHOULD TAKE A DIFFERENT ROUTE BACK, SEE IF WE CAN FIND ANY SUPPLIES.
EVERYONE UP FOR THAT?

I'M FINE, SO YEAH... THAT'S A GOOD IDEA.
COME ON.

ARE YOU MAD AT ME?

I'M NOT AS MAD AS I AM RELIEVED THAT YOU'RE ALIVE.
WE'LL TALK, BUT I WON'T YELL... MUCH.

THIS PLACE IS UNBELIEVABLE!

WHAT IS IT?

IT HAS ABSOLUTELY EVERYTHING I NEED. THE OWNER MUST HAVE BEEN MAKING HIS OWN BULLETS ON THE SIDE.
THEY EVEN HAVE A SWAGING PRESS FOR CHRIST'S SAKE!

YEAH... WHATEVER THAT IS.

IT'S A PRESS THAT MAKES METAL FORMS BY PUSHING METAL THROUGH DIES--IT DOESN'T MATTER, IT MEANS WE WON'T HAVE TO DO A LOT OF CASTING AND WE CAN WORK WITH METAL AT ROOM TEMPERATURE.
IT'LL MAKE THINGS EASIER.

THAT LAST PART I UNDERSTOOD.

THIS GUY EVEN HAS A STOCKPILE OF PRIMER THAT'LL PROBABLY GET US THROUGH A COUPLE OF BATCHES.
TECHNICAL... SORRY.

THIS PLACE IS SOMETHING ELSE... WE GET A BUNCH OF PEOPLE WORKING IN HERE... WE CAN MAKE A LOT MORE THAN BULLETS.
ASSUMING ANYONE ACTUALLY KNOWS HOW TO USE THIS CRAP.

THEY'VE ALREADY GOT THINGS SET UP FOR NINE MILLIMETER BULLETS AND A COUPLE OTHERS.
I'LL GET AN ACCOUNTING FROM OLIVIA ON WHICH GUNS WE HAVE THE MOST OF, TO SEE WHAT AMMUNITION WOULD BE THE MOST USEFUL TO PRODUCE.

GOOD FIND, EUGENE.
NICE JOB.

OH... THANKS.
JUST, UM... DOING MY PART.

I KNOW WE'RE ALL EXCITED TO SEE CARL BACK SAFE AND SOUND, BUT THERE'S A LOT OF WORK TO BE DONE.

OLIVIA, I NEED YOU TO WORK WITH ANDREA TO GET ALL THE SUPPLIES WE PICKED UP TODAY CATALOGUED AND SEPARATED. WE NEED TO STORE THE SAVIORS' CUT FOR WHEN THEY COME TO PICK IT UP.
NEGAN SPARED MY SON. HE WANTED TO SHOW HE CAN BE REASONABLE... I'M TAKING THE GESTURE AT FACE VALUE.
IT MAKES ME FEEL LIKE HE CAN BE TRUSTED AND I HAVE MADE THE RIGHT DECISION. LET'S ALL HOPE THAT'S ACTUALLY THE CASE.

THIS WILL BE TOUGH ON US MOVING FORWARD, BUT IT WILL BE WORTH IT IN THE END.
THANK YOU FOR CONTINUING TO TRUST ME. I BELIEVE WE CAN DO GREAT THINGS BY WORKING TOGETHER AS WE HAVE.
I TRULY BELIEVE THINGS WILL CONTINUE TO GET BETTER FROM HERE ON OUT... IT'S TIME TO BE *OPTIMISTIC.*

LAID IT ON THERE A BIT THICK AT THE END, DON'T YOU THINK?

THAT WAS THE ONLY PART THAT WAS SINCERE. I DO BELIEVE THAT THINGS WILL GET BETTER.
ESPECIALLY ONCE WE HAVE NEGAN OUT OF THE PICTURE.

THAT'S WHAT I'M TALKING ABOUT. I UNDERSTAND THE REASON FOR KEEPING EVERYONE ELSE IN THE DARK, BUT I FEAR YOU MIGHT BE GOING TOO FAR.
YOU'RE LYING TO THEM. THEY'RE PROBABLY NOT GOING TO BE TOO HAPPY WHEN THEY SEE HOW FAR YOU'VE GONE TO TRICK THEM.

BUT THEY'LL BE ALIVE.
I DON'T CARE ABOUT THE REST. THEY'LL GET OVER IT.

I HOPE YOU'RE RIGHT.

YOU THINK HE'S OKAY?
I'M GOING TO TALK TO HIM TONIGHT.

HUH?

MY SHIFT'S NOT OVER FOR ANOTHER HOUR-- AND YOU'RE NOT THE ONE WHO'S RELIEVING ME.

SOMETHING HAPPEN BETWEEN YOU AND DENISE?
WHY ARE YOU SPENDING MOST OF YOUR NIGHTS ON WATCH DUTY?

UH...

PLEASE.
DON'T DO THIS, MICHONNE.

MAGGIE TOLD ME ABOUT YOU AND TYREESE.
I DON'T KNOW WHERE I SIT WITH DENISE RIGHT NOW, WE'RE FIGURING THINGS OUT. AND I'M NOT GOING TO SCREW THAT UP, OKAY?

I DON'T KNOW WHAT IT IS-- SOMETHING WHERE YOU NEED TO SHOW YOU'RE BETTER THAN OTHER WOMEN BY GETTING SOMEONE WHO'S UNAVAILABLE... IT'S JUST NOT... NECESSARY.
YOU'RE BEAUTIFUL... IF THINGS GO SOUTH WITH DENISE, SURE. BUT... HAVE SOME SELF-RESPECT.

IF YOU'RE LONELY... AND HOW COULD YOU NOT BE... JUST DON'T BE SO DAMN STAND-OFFISH.
IT'S OFF-PUTTING.

THINGS ARE DIFFERENT NOW. YOU DON'T HAVE TO BE ON GUARD.
WE'RE ALL IN THIS TOGETHER. YOU--

THAT'S ENOUGH.
THIS DIDN'T HAPPEN.

I'M SORRY.

WATER?
I'M FINE, THANKS.

WHAT DID CARL HAVE TO SAY? ANYTHING USEFUL?
THINK SO.
THANKS.

YOU KNOW ANYTHING ABOUT NEGAN'S "WIVES?" APPARENTLY HE LIVES WITH FIVE WOMEN IN SOME PENTHOUSE HE'S SET UP IN THE TOP FLOOR OF THAT FACTORY.
CARL HAD A LOT TO SAY ABOUT THEM. APPARENTLY THEY PARADE AROUND HALF NAKED ALL DAY.

THAT'S NEWS TO ME.
WE HAD NO IDEA WHERE THE PLACE WAS UNTIL RECENTLY... LET ALONE WHAT GOES ON INSIDE, OR HOW MANY PEOPLE LIVE THERE.

WELL, THAT'S THE INTERESTING PART. CARL SAYS HE SAW AT LEAST THIRTY PEOPLE WHILE HE WAS THERE. COULD BE MORE.
THING IS, HE SAYS THEY'RE NORMAL PEOPLE, MEN, WOMEN... SOME KIDS. THEY'RE NOT ALL SOLDIERS. HE SAID MOST OF THEM ARE JUST REGULAR PEOPLE.
NOT MANY FIGHTERS.

THAT MAKES SENSE. NEGAN HAS A FEW OUTPOSTS, LIKE HE'S ESTABLISHED SOME KIND OF PERIMETER, A SAFE ZONE-- THOUGH IT'S NOT EXACTLY SAFE.
HE KEEPS PEOPLE STATIONED AT THOSE. ONCE HE'S NO LONGER INTERESTED IN GETTING A PEEK INSIDE HERE-- HE'LL HAVE YOU START HAULING YOUR GOODS TO DROP POINTS, CLOSER TO THOSE OUTPOSTS.
SO HE'S GOT MORE SOLDIERS... WE JUST NEVER KNEW WHAT WAS BACK AT WHERE THEY LIVED--OR EVEN IF THEY LIVED IN A FIXED PLACE.
THIS IS ALL USEFUL.

CARL DIDN'T SEE ANY GUNS. NO STOCKPILES OF AMMUNITION.
SEEMS LIKE THEY'RE TAPPED.
WE'VE SUSPECTED THAT FOR A LONG TIME. WE DON'T REALLY RELY ON FIREARMS THAT MUCH AT THE HILLTOP EITHER. THAT STUFF IS SCARCE.
DON'T KNOW HOW YOU'VE STAYED SO WELL-STOCKED FOR SO LONG.

WE'VE BEEN LUCKY.

SO WE KNOW WHERE THE SAVIORS LIVE... AND THAT IT'S NOT FILLED TO THE BRIM WITH SOLDIERS...

WHAT? JESUS, WHAT IS IT?
I THINK IT'S TIME I INTRODUCE YOU TO **EZEKIEL.**

LET THE SLAUGHTER BEGIN!

ZERO SERVING ZERO.
GET FUCKING READY.

ANYONE LAYING DOWN BETS?
THOK!

OH, NICE ONE. THREE SERVING ONE.

MY SERVE. NINE SERVING ONE.

DID I LOSE TRACK, OR IS THIS GAME POINT?
TWENTY SERVING FOUR.

THAT'S GAME!
FUCK YES, MOTHER-FUCKERS!

DWIGHT. YOU WANT TO JUMP IN HERE-- SHOW ME WHAT YOU'VE GOT BEFORE YOU HIT THE ROAD?

THANKS, BUT NO. I REALLY SHOULD BE GOING.

OH, FINE... GO. ANYONE ELSE?
ANYONE? OKAY THEN.
BUNCH OF WIMPS.

WAS GETTING BORING ANYWAY.
NOW IF YOU'LL EXCUSE ME, I'M GOING TO GO PING PONG MY DICK ALL OVER THESE TITTIES!
CATCH YOU LATER, DWIGHT.

SHIT, I DIDN'T KNOW THERE WERE THIS MANY OUT HERE.
PIECE OF CAKE.

CARL, RUN INSIDE BEFORE THEY BLOCK THE WAY-- GO!
SVAASH!

AND LEAVE YOU HERE-- NO WAY!
I CAN HANDLE THIS.

BLAM!

I'LL FOLLOW RIGHT BEHIND YOU! YOU WON'T LEAVE ME! WE CAN GATHER MORE PEOPLE AND COME BACK!
SVAASH!
DAMN IT, CARL, DON'T MAKE ME DRAG YOU INSIDE!

NO WAY! WE CAN DO THIS!
THERE'S NOT THAT MANY!
BLAM!

SEE?!
WE GOT THIS!

GRUAH!
YEAAGH!!

NO!
NO!

CARL!

AGH!
UMPH!

BLAM!

GUH.

SVAASH!

DAMN IT, CARL!

MY HAT!

WE'LL COME BACK FOR IT LATER!

UNGH.
DAMN IT.

ARE YOU OKAY?

THEY ALMOST GOT ME.
I ALMOST DIED.

IT'S NOT A GAME OUT THERE. DID YOU FORGET THAT? YOU DON'T GET COMFORTABLE.
YOU DON'T RELAX WHILE YOU'RE OUT THERE. IT ONLY TAKES A SECOND... ONE FALSE MOVE...
...AND IT'S OVER.

IT WAS MY EYE... MY BLIND SPOT.
I CAN HOLD MY OWN, I WOULD HAVE BEEN FINE... I COULDN'T... SEE IT... THE ONE THAT ATTACKED ME.

I'M WORTHLESS NOW.
STOP THAT RIGHT NOW. YOU DON'T FEEL SORRY FOR YOURSELF.

YOUR DAD IS MISSING A HAND. HE DOES JUST FINE. YOU DEAL WITH YOUR LIMITATIONS.
YOU'LL LEARN-- YOU'LL GET USED TO IT. YOU'RE STRONG, CARL. EVERYONE CAN SEE THAT.
NOW, GET A KNIFE--HELP ME STAB THESE ROAMERS THROUGH THE FENCE. AND... WHEN YOUR DAD GETS BACK, THIS STAYS BETWEEN US.
OKAY...

YOU KNOW THIS EZEKIEL?
HE'S PART OF THE NETWORK, WITH THE HILLTOP AND THE SAVIORS, ALTHOUGH I HAVE A HARD TIME INCLUDING THEM IN OUR GROUP. THEY'RE MORE A TUMOR THAN A PARTICIPANT.
THERE ARE A COUPLE OTHER SMALLER GROUPS WE KNOW OF... BUT WE DON'T REALLY ENGAGE THEM MUCH.
THE KINGDOM IS THE BIGGEST SETTLEMENT WE KNOW OF OUTSIDE OF THE HILLTOP.

THE KINGDOM?
YEAH. LOOK, MAN. I DIDN'T NAME IT.

WELL, HOW MUCH LONGER UNTIL WE REACH THIS "KINGDOM"?
TECHNICALLY WE'RE ALREADY HERE, AT THE OUTERMOST EDGE.

THEN WHAT ARE WE WAITING ON?
THEM.

WHO DARES TRESPASS ON THE SOVEREIGN LAND OF--
OH, SHIT-- JESUS? IS THAT YOU?!

HOT DAMN, MAN. WE DIDN'T RECOGNIZE YOU AT FIRST. SORRY IF WE STARTLED YOU.
WHO'S YOUR FRIEND?

THIS IS RICK GRIMES, LEADER OF A LIKE-MINDED COMMUNITY. WE... REQUEST AN AUDIENCE WITH KING EZEKIEL.

ABSOLUTELY. HE'LL BE THRILLED TO SEE YOU.
THIS WAY.

"KING EZEKIEL?"
JUST GO WITH IT.
AND FOR FUTURE REFERENCE, YOU NEVER ENTER THE KINGDOM WITHOUT AN ESCORT.

NO CARS INSIDE THE WALL-- C'MON.

WHERE IS EVERYONE?

THEY LIVE INSIDE THE SCHOOL TOGETHER IN THE WINTER, BUT SPREAD OUT TO THESE TENTS WHEN IT WARMS UP.

YOU WILL WAIT HERE UNTIL OUR KING CAN ADDRESS YOU.

JESUS, MY FRIEND!

IT PLEASES ME TO SEE YOU, OLD FRIEND.
TELL ME, WHAT NEWS DO YOU BRING GOOD KING EZEKIEL? IS THIS A NEW ALLY YOU'VE BROUGHT ME?

INDEED IT IS, YOUR MAJESTY. THIS IS--
UH...

OH, I THINK I FORGOT TO MENTION...
EZEKIEL HAS A TIGER.

SOMETIMES I STILL STOP AND THINK, I'M HAVING LUNCH WITH A FRIEND RIGHT NOW. WE'RE SITTING AT A TABLE, LOOKING AT EACH OTHER, EATING.
I'M ALMOST CERTAIN WE WON'T BE ATTACKED BEFORE WE FINISH THIS MEAL.
THERE WAS A TIME THAT WAS NOT THE CASE.

I DON'T EVER WANT TO FORGET THAT. I DON'T EVER WANT TO TAKE THAT FOR GRANTED.

MICHONNE? YOU LISTENING?

THIS ISN'T ME.

I CAN'T *TALK* TO PEOPLE ANYMORE. I HAVE NO SOCIAL GRACES. LAST NIGHT, WITH HEATH, I--
I'M EMBARRASSED TO EVEN SAY IT.
THIS IS NOT WHO I AM. I USED TO BE TALKATIVE AND FRIENDLY EVEN FUN...

...AND I DON'T THINK I CAN EVER GO BACK TO THAT.

GOOD AFTERNOON, SPENCER. WHAT CAN I DO FOR YOU?
NOTHING, UH... FATHER GABRIEL... I WAS WONDERING IF I COULD JUST HAVE A MINUTE ON THE ALTAR...

OF COURSE. GO RIGHT AHEAD.

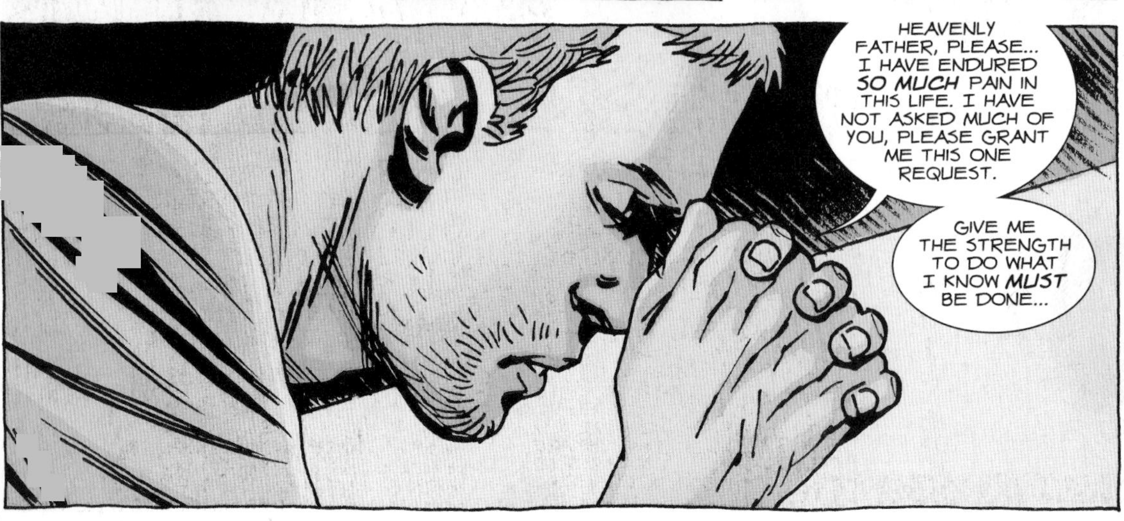
HEAVENLY FATHER, PLEASE... I HAVE ENDURED SO MUCH PAIN IN THIS LIFE. I HAVE NOT ASKED MUCH OF YOU, PLEASE GRANT ME THIS ONE REQUEST.
GIVE ME THE STRENGTH TO DO WHAT I KNOW MUST BE DONE...

GREGORY ON HIS HILLTOP... SUCH A COWARD. HE HAS MORE PEOPLE THAN ALL OF US, HE COULD HAVE AN ARMY, INSTEAD HE SPENDS HIS TIME COWERING IN HIS BIG HOUSE, TRYING TO HIDE THE FACT THAT HE'S SO SCARED.
I'VE NEVER SEEN SOMEONE GO SO FAR SIMPLY ON THE POWER OF HIS LIES.

NO, I HAVE NEVER BEEN ACCEPTING OF NEGAN'S TRUCE. I CROWNED MYSELF KING OF THIS KINGDOM IN ORDER TO MAKE THE LIVES OF MY PEOPLE AS GOOD AS THEY CAN BE.
NEGAN AND HIS SAVIORS... I WISH TO BE RID OF THEM. YOUR FRIEND JESUS KNOWS HOW DEEP MY HATRED FOR THESE PEOPLE BURNS, HOW I'VE SIMPLY BEEN WAITING FOR THE RIGHT MOMENT TO STRIKE AGAINST THESE DEVILS.
YOUR SON'S EXPERIENCE PROVIDES ME WITH MORE THAN ENOUGH INFORMATION NEEDED TO LAUNCH AN ASSAULT. I THANK YOU AND AGAIN, I AM TRULY SORRY FOR WHAT HE HAD TO ENDURE TO RETRIEVE THAT INFORMATION.

I HAVE MANY PEOPLE IN MY COMMUNITY WHO WOULD BE WILLING TO HELP YOU IN THAT ASSAULT. I DON'T EXPECT YOU TO FIGHT MY BATTLES FOR ME.
I ONLY ASK FOR YOUR HELP.

AND YOU HAVE IT, RICK GRIMES.
THE DAY HAS FINALLY COME TO RIGHT THE WRONGS THAT HAVE BEFALLEN SO MANY PEOPLE UNDER THIS TYRANT.

I AM PLEASED TO REPORT THAT FATE HAS BROUGHT MANY TRAVELERS TO THE KINGDOM, MY KINGDOM, TODAY.
TRAVELERS WITH A SINGULAR PURPOSE. YOUR ARRIVAL CAN BE NO COINCIDENCE-- IT MUST BE A SIGN THAT WE ARE DESTINED TO SUCCEED IN OUR TASK.

MAKE YOUR PRESENCE KNOWN, TRAVELER.

I GET THAT I'M PROBABLY THE SECOND TO LAST PERSON YOU'D EVER WANT TO SEE, BUT YOU NEED TO UNDERSTAND SOMETHING.
IT APPEARS I'VE HAD A CHANGE OF HEART, BUT I ASSURE YOU, I'VE NEVER BEEN FULLY IN SUPPORT OF NEGAN.

I DON'T BELIEVE THIS MOTHERFUCKER FOR A SECOND.
I'VE **SEEN** HIM CARRY OUT NEGAN'S WISHES. HE'S **KILLED** MEN ON NEGAN'S BEHALF. HE'S ONE OF HIS LIEUTENANTS.
IF HE'S SAYING HE'S WITH US--**HE'S LYING.**

THAT WHAT YOU THINK'S GOING ON HERE? THAT I **KNEW** YOU WERE GOING TO SHOW UP AND I WANTED TO TRICK YOU INTO REVEALING YOUR PLAN BY COMING TO A PLACE I DIDN'T EVEN THINK YOU **KNEW ABOUT?**
I THOUGHT YOU WERE UNDER NEGAN'S SPELL LIKE THE REST. EZEKIEL'S THE ONLY ONE I KNEW HAD ANY KIND OF BALLS TO FACE NEGAN... MAKE A MOVE AGAINST HIM.
I'M HERE TO HELP MAKE THAT HAPPEN. I CAN TELL YOU **EVERYTHING.** I CAN MAKE YOUR LITTLE PLAN POSSIBLE.

EZEKIEL, HEAR ME OUT. IF NEGAN GAVE ME MY SON BACK--KNOWING CARL'D GIVE US INFORMATION ABOUT HIS FACTORY... AND HE KNEW THAT YOU HAD PLANS TO MOVE AGAINST HIM...
...IT'S AT LEAST POSSIBLE THAT HE WOULD KNOW JESUS WOULD BRING ME TO YOU--TO TRY AND MOUNT SOME KIND OF ATTACK AGAINST HIM, SEEING AS WE'RE THE TWO GROUPS WHO COULD DO IT.

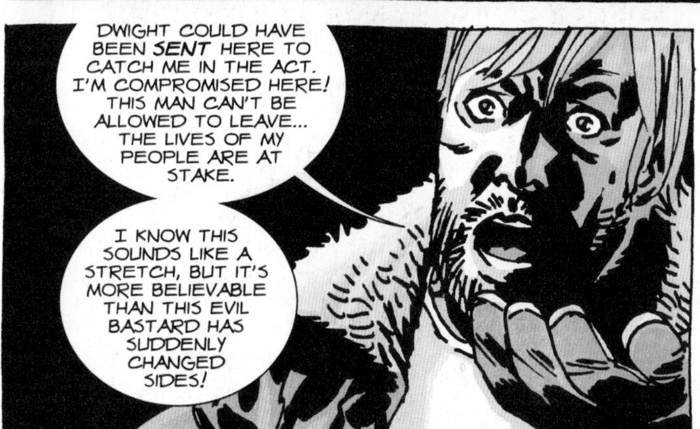
DWIGHT COULD HAVE BEEN SENT HERE TO CATCH ME IN THE ACT. I'M COMPROMISED HERE! THIS MAN CAN'T BE ALLOWED TO LEAVE... THE LIVES OF MY PEOPLE ARE AT STAKE.
I KNOW THIS SOUNDS LIKE A STRETCH, BUT IT'S MORE BELIEVABLE THAN THIS EVIL BASTARD HAS SUDDENLY CHANGED SIDES!

NEGAN HAS MY WIFE! I HAD TO DO AS HE ASKED OR HE'D HURT HER!
YOU THINK YOU'VE PUT MORE ON THE LINE?!
YOU HAVE NO IDEA WHAT I'VE RISKED COMING HERE--WHAT HE'S CAPABLE OF. YOU THINK YOU'VE GOT MORE TO LOSE THAN I DO?!

LIAR!
WRAKK!

ROAARRR!!

DOOM! DOOM!

PLEASE ACCEPT MY APOLOGIES. SHIVA ABHORS VIOLENCE.

AS DO I.

YOUR SON... HE TELL YOU ABOUT NEGAN'S WIVES? THE FIRST ONE HE TOOK, THE DARK-HAIRED ONE. MIGHT HAVE DESCRIBED HER AS THE NICE ONE.
THAT WAS MY WIFE SHERRY.
SHE... CHOSE IT, THOUGHT IT'D MAKE OUR LIVES EASIER. WE DIDN'T REALIZE HOW MUCH WE NEEDED EACH OTHER UNTIL WE WERE APART. THING IS... ONCE IT'S DECIDED... THERE'S NO GOING BACK.
HE CAUGHT US TOGETHER.

THAT'S WHEN HE DID THIS TO ME.

AFTER THAT, I NEVER DID ANYTHING HE DIDN'T ASK ME TO. I NEVER DISOBEYED HIM, I WAS A GOOD SOLDIER, I DID AS I WAS TOLD.
I WAS A COWARD.
AND I DID A LOT OF TERRIBLE THINGS I CAN'T TAKE BACK.

BUT I CAN HELP YOU END HIS REIGN OF TERROR... FREE ALL THE PEOPLE EXISTING UNDER HIS THRALL.
I CAN MAKE THINGS RIGHT. IF YOU'LL JUST TRUST ME.

I'LL TELL YOU HIS SECRETS, HIS WEAKNESSES... I'LL BRING YOU THAT ASSHOLE'S HEAD ON A SILVER PLATTER...
...AND THEN IT WON'T MATTER IF YOU TRUST ME... BECAUSE THAT MOTHERFUCKER WILL BE DEAD.
AND THIS NIGHTMARE WILL, AT LONG LAST, BE OVER.

MARION COUNTY PUBLIC LIBRARY
321 MONROE STREET
FAIRMONT, WV 26554

TO BE CONTINUED...

FOR MORE OF THE WALKING DEAD

TRADE PAPERBACKS

VOL. 1: DAYS GONE BYE TP
ISBN: 978-1-58240-672-5
$14.99

VOL. 2: MILES BEHIND US TP
ISBN: 978-1-58240-775-3
$14.99

VOL. 3: SAFETY BEHIND BARS TP
ISBN: 978-1-58240-805-7
$14.99

VOL. 4: THE HEART'S DESIRE TP
ISBN: 978-1-58240-530-8
$14.99

VOL. 5: THE BEST DEFENSE TP
ISBN: 978-1-58240-612-1
$14.99

VOL. 6: THIS SORROWFUL LIFE TP
ISBN: 978-1-58240-684-8
$14.99

VOL. 7: THE CALM BEFORE TP
ISBN: 978-1-58240-828-6
$14.99

VOL. 8: MADE TO SUFFER TP
ISBN: 978-1-58240-883-5
$14.99

VOL. 9: HERE WE REMAIN TP
ISBN: 978-1-60706-022-2
$14.99

VOL. 10: WHAT WE BECOME TP
ISBN: 978-1-60706-075-8
$14.99

VOL. 11: FEAR THE HUNTERS TP
ISBN: 978-1-60706-181-6
$14.99

VOL. 12: LIFE AMONG THEM TP
ISBN: 978-1-60706-254-7
$14.99

VOL. 13: TOO FAR GONE TP
ISBN: 978-1-60[illegible]6-3[illegible]
$14.99

VOL. 14: NO WAY [illegible]
ISBN: 978-1-60706-392-6
$14.99

VOL. 15: WE FIND OURSELVES TP
ISBN: 978-1-60706-44[illegible]
$14.99

VOL. 16: A LARGER WORLD [illegible]
ISBN: 978-1-60706-559[illegible]
$14.99

VOL. 17: SOMET[illegible] FEAR TP
ISBN: 978-1-6070[illegible]15-6
$14.99

VOL. 18: [illegible] TP
ISBN: 978-1-60706-687-3
$14.99

HARDCOVERS

BOOK ONE HC
ISBN: 978-1-58240-619-0
$34.99

BOOK TWO HC
ISBN: 978-1-58240-698-5
$34.99

BOOK THREE HC
ISBN: 978-1-58240-825-5
$34.99

BOOK FOUR HC
ISBN: 978-1-60706-000-0
$34.99

BOOK FIVE HC
ISBN: 978-1-60706-171-7
$34.99

BOOK SIX HC
ISBN: 978-1-60706-327-8
$34.99

BOOK SEVEN HC
ISBN: 978-1-60706-439-8
$34.99

BOOK EIGHT HC
ISBN: 978-1-60706-593-7
$34.99

COMPENDIUMS

COMPENDIUM TP, VOL. 1
ISBN: 978-1-60706-076-5
$59.99

COMPENDIUM TP, VOL. 2
ISBN: 978-1-60706-596-8
$59.99

SPECIALTY BOOKS

THE WALKING DEAD: THE COVERS, VOL. 1 H[illegible]
ISBN: 978-1-60706-002-4
$24.99

THE WALKING DEAD SURVIVORS' GUIDE
ISBN: 978-1-60706-458-9
$12.99

OMNIBUS

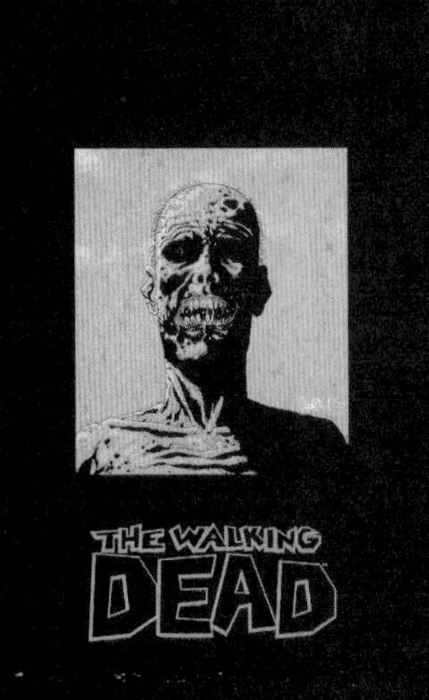

OMNIBUS, VOL. 1
ISBN: 978-1-60706-503-[illegible]
$100.00

OMNIBUS, VOL. 2
ISBN: 978-1-60706-51[illegible]
$100.00

OMNIBUS, VOL. 3
ISBN: 978-1-60706-330-8
$100.00

OMNIBUS, VOL. 4
ISBN: 978-1-60706-616-3
$100.00